SWIMMER IN THE SECRET SEA

novella by

{ William Kotzwinkle }

SWIMMER IN THE SECRET SEA

CHRONICLE BOOKS
SAN FRANCISCO

This work originally appeared
in slightly different form in *Redbook* magazine
and appears in *Prize Stories 1975: The O. Henry Awards.*

First hardcover edition 1994
Printed in the United States of America

Library of Congress Cataloging-in-Publication Data
Kotzwinkle, William.
Swimmer in the secret sea : novella / by William Kotzwinkle.
—first hardcover edition.
p. cm.
ISBN 0-8118-0715-0 (hc)
1. Marriage—United States—Fiction.
2. Infants (Newborn)—Death—Fiction. I. Title.
PS3561.085S9 1994
813'.54—dc20   93-43660
CIP

Cover design: Gretchen Scoble and Diane Kasprowicz
Book typography: Diane Kasprowicz
Composition: Not Your Type, New Haven CT
Cover photograph: Mark Dauber

Distributed in Canada by Raincoast Books
112 East Third Avenue
Vancouver, BC V5T 1C8

10 9 8 7 6 5 4 3 2 1

CHRONICLE BOOKS
275 Fifth Street
San Francisco, CA 94103

SWIMMER IN THE SECRET SEA

JOHNNY, MY WATER just broke!"

Laski rose through a sea of dreams, trying to find the surface. The sea was dark, and iridescent creatures came toward him, one of them suddenly exploding into brilliance. Laski woke, sitting up in bed. Diane had her hand on the night lamp and was staring down at a water stain spreading on the sheets.

"That's it," he said. "Get ready." The first wave of shock was already over him, speeding his pulse, turning his skin cold, making him shiver.

"I'd better put a napkin on," she said. "I'm getting everything all wet."

He took her arm and helped her to the stairs. She too had begun to tremble and they were trembling together as they passed the window and saw the forest, covered with snow. The stillness of the woods calmed him, and he paused with her on the landing, drinking in the white nectar of the moon. His trembling subsided some, but hers continued, and he walked with her toward the bathroom. She went stooped over, her arms across her mountainous stomach, where her earthquake had its origin. He helped her onto the toilet seat, then went to the closet and brought a blanket. He wrapped it around her and rubbed his hands up and down her arms, trying to generate some warmth.

She looked up at him, her teeth chattering. He hadn't expected it to be like this, the two of them caught and shaken like rag dolls. They'd studied the childbirth manuals carefully, and performed the exercises regularly, and he'd thought it would be merely an extension of all that, but there'd been no transition. Suddenly they were being dragged over a bed of rocks. Her eyes were like a child's, astonished and terrified, but her voice was calm and he realized she was prepared, in spite of fear and chattering teeth.

"I can control the water now," she said. "I can keep it from running out."

"I'll get the truck warmed up." He went outside into the snow. Beyond the shadowy tops of the pines the vast sky-bowl glittered, and the half-ton truck sat in the moonlight, covered with brightly sparkling ice. He opened the door and slid in, pulling on the choke and turning the ignition key.

The starter motor whined, caught in the icy hand of the North. "Come on," said Laski softly, appealing to the finer nature of the truck, the trusty half-ton which never failed him. He listened for the little cough of life in the whining, and when it came he quickly gunned the motor, bringing the truck completely to life. "You're a good old wagon." As far north as they were, any motor could freeze up, any battery suddenly die, and it was fifteen miles through the thickest forest to the nearest other vehicle. He'd seen fires built under motors, and had heard incredible cursing float out on northern nights, while hours had passed and all ideas had failed and nobody went anywhere. He kept the choke out, so the motor ran fast, then turned on the heater and stepped back out into the snow. The truck's exhaust was the only cloud against the brilliant moon, and he went through the swirling vapor, back toward the cabin which sat like a tiny lantern in the great tangled wilderness.

Diane was still shivering in the bathroom, her stomach bulging under her nightgown. He helped her back toward the stairs, and up to the bedroom, where she started to dress, going through all the regular motions, but trembling constantly. It seemed to Laski there were two distinct Dianes—one who was shaking like a leaf, and another who was as calm and decisive as any old midwife. He felt the same split in himself as he picked up her valise and carried it toward the stairs. His hand was trembling, his heart pounding, but another part of him was calm, unshakable as an old tree. This calm quiet partner seemed to dwell in some region of the body Laski couldn't identify. His guts were jumping, his brain was racing, his legs were shaking, but somewhere in him there was peace.

He stepped into the snow. The truck was running smoothly now and he eased off on the choke, until the engine was gently cooking. Turning, he saw Diane through the upstairs window of the cabin, her stomach huge in front of her. She moved slowly and carefully, and he knew that she was going to exactly the clothes she'd planned on, finding them just where she wanted them. His own life was a bundle of clothes flung in all directions, shoes dancing in unlikely places, nothing where he could find it.

He went back in, joining her in the bathroom. "How're you feeling?"

"The contractions have begun."

"What are they like?"

"I can't describe it."

He helped her down the stairs to the door, and looked around the kitchen. She's got everything in place, there's no more to be done here. He locked the door behind him and led her to the truck.

She slid inside and he covered her with a blanket.

The truck was warm and moved easily up the snow-packed lane, through the tall pine trees. At the top of the lane he turned onto the narrow road. They'd walked it all winter long, and they'd played a game, pretending that the baby had already been born and was swinging along between them like a little trapeze artist holding onto their hands, and they'd swung him that way, up and down the road.

The road went past a vast snow-covered field, in which an old wagon appeared, on its own journey to nowhere, rotting away, its spoked wheels half-buried in the snow.

"I'd feel better if you didn't go so fast."

He slowed down. One minute, ten minutes saved, makes no difference. We know how long the first stages of labor last.

There was ice beneath the snow, and the wheels of the truck did not have perfect traction, but he knew how to play the road, easing through the turns, never using much brake. Both sides of the narrow road had been deeply ditched to carry away the waters of the spring runoff, but now they were covered with snow and it would be a simple matter to slide into the ditch and be there all night. Every winter he'd helped pull travelers out of the ditch, with much swearing, skidding, heaving, and hauling. It was great fun; but not tonight.

At the bend in the road stood the one-room schoolhouse, forgotten in the moonlight. He geared down, taking the turn in second, thinking of little boys with caps and knickers on, and little girls in gingham dresses, long ago, coming up the hill toward the schoolhouse. Then he was through the turn, leaving the old ghosts behind him, on their endless walk through a buried century.

The road went straight through pines which formed a high wall on both sides. "Old Ben is up," said Laski, nodding toward a ramshackle farmhouse in the midst of the trees. Most of the windows were broken out and it was like all the other abandoned farmhouses in the settlement, except for a flickering light inside, from the one room the old lumberjack had sealed off against the elements.

Diane looked toward the light. A hermit herself, she liked old Ben. He had a bad reputation in the village, living as he did, so contrary to the ways of the world. But he could make anything out of wood —fiddles, boats, snowshoes—and he'd spent a lifetime in the woods. Laski saw a shadow moving in the darkness—old Ben's dog, sniffing around in the snow. Then the truck was into the next turn, near the river that came out of the darkness, its icy skin shining in the moonlight. Laski followed the river until it slipped back into the trees, where it wove a silver thread through the dark branches.

Another clearing appeared, and a small board shack. It was a camp for "sports," as the backwoods Canadians called the Americans who came to fish and hunt and rough it for a week. Laski remembered a time, a long time ago—he and his father were fishing in Canada, steering a motorboat along on a bright morning over a wide and winding river. Laski had suddenly felt like he was the river and the trees and the sun and the wind.

He touched Diane gently on the shoulder. She

was trembling inside her heavy coat, and he knew enough not to ask her how she felt.

The camp for American sports fell back into darkness. The villagers had thought of Laski and his wife as sports, with no visible means of support, until it was learned they were artists. Never having had such strange creatures around, except for old Coleman Johns, the mad inventor who had built his own automatic milking machine and promised to make a trip to the moon with a magnet in his pants, the country people left the Laskis alone. There was some talk that Laski, with his thick beard and wire glasses, resembled old Coleman enough to be his twin brother. Whenever Laski drove past the ruined foundation that had once been Coleman's home, he was overtaken by a strange nostalgia, as if he and the mad inventor had shared the same vision of this vast land, which made men build strange objects beneath the moon.

Laski's sculpture was certainly odd. Likenesses of Diane filled the forest, her strangely beautiful face gradually appearing on tree stumps or on rocks.

Old dead trees with gray bare branches had become Diane dancing, like a priestess of the wood. Eventually the ceaseless weaving of the weeds had made gowns of green for the statues, bright berry beads and buttons entwining the arms and legs, marking them as part of the endless dream of the deep pines.

"The contractions are ten minutes apart."

Laski laid a firmer foot on the gas petal. Baby's in a hurry.

A ghostly light flashed ahead of Laski, leaping out of the darkness of the country graveyard where Coleman Johns lay buried and where Laski's headlights had caught the top of an old tombstone. The truck wheels spun on the turn, rear end lashing like a tail before coming straight again. Then darkness claimed the graveyard once more and the road was again lined by heavy forest.

MATERNITY?" SMILED THE receptionist. "Do you have your papers with you?"

Diane took them out of her purse. An orderly came across the waiting room with a wheelchair and Diane sat down in it, still wearing her shaggy forest coat. Laski looked at the receptionist.

"The orderly will take her up and you can follow in just a few minutes, sir. I have some papers for you to fill out."

Laski touched Diane's hand, and she looked at him, smiling but distant, as the orderly turned the chair and wheeled her off.

The receptionist put a form into her typewriter
and asked Laski questions about age, address, insur-
ance—lifeless items holding him in his chair.

A drunken young man, face cut and swollen,
swaggered into the waiting room. Glassy-eyed, he
approached the desk. The receptionist looked up. "If
you'll have a seat please," she said coldly.

The young man leaned on the desk, but the receptionist ignored him, even though he was bleed-
ing from a wound over his eye.

Laski looked into the young man's eyes, expecting hostility. He found a frightened child making
brave. The nurses will give him a hard time, thought
Laski. Then the doctor will stitch him and he'll be
turned back out into the night. But he was once the
baby on the way and everybody rallied around him.
The great moment was once his.

An older man entered the waiting room and
looked around for a moment, until his eye caught
the young man's figure. He came over slowly, his
walk and manner similar to the young man's.

"What happened?"

"Nothing much," said the young man, striking a confident pose.

"I haven't seen you for awhile."

"I've been around."

"You interested in working?"

"Yeah, sure."

"You can go to work tomorrow."

"Oh no," said the young man, shaking his head and touching his bruises. "I can't do anything tomorrow."

The papers were completed. The orderly returned and Laski followed him down the hallway to an elevator. They rode together in silence, to the floor marked MATERNITY. The hall held a couch and two leather chairs. Beyond it was a door marked DELIVERY—NO ADMITTANCE.

The orderly walked away. Laski sat down. This is where all the fathers wait. He stood, and walked slowly up and down. Now I'm pacing the floor like an expectant father.

The sounds of a floor-waxing machine came along the hallway, somewhere out of sight, whirring, wheels creaking, coming along. Laski listened to its approach and then it appeared, pushed along by a uniformed maintenance man. "This is your big night, eh?"

"Yes."

The waxer nodded and waxed on. He's seen it all, thought Laski, seen them come and go, seen them every night—pacing back and forth on his waxed floor.

An elderly nurse came out of the delivery room. Laski looked at her, but she gave him such a blank cold stare all questions dissolved in his throat. He listened to her footsteps going away down the hall, and then he walked over and peered through the porthole window in the delivery room door. The hall beyond the porthole was dimly lit and empty.

He paced back again, past the leather chairs. The alcohol-medicine smell of the hospital filled the air. The floor was squared tile; he stepped between the cracks with each foot. His boots were still wet with snow. The dark tips of them looked back at him, worn down and scarred from the forest.

He reined himself around, came back the other way along the floor. The door swung open again. A young nurse appeared, smiling. "We're just getting your wife ready," she said. "You'll be able to join her in a few minutes."

DIANE WAS SITTING up in bed. He went quickly to her, searching her eyes, which showed the same mixture of fear and calm he'd seen all night.

"The baby's upside-down," she said.

The air seemed dreamlike, a dream in which he could make things take any shape he liked. But he was standing in a hospital room and their baby was upside-down. "It'll be all right," he said, touching her folded hands.

"Doctor Barker says he doesn't want you in on a breech birth. I told him I understand, and that I hope he'll change his mind."

Her face suddenly changed as the contraction came on and she began her breathing as they'd practiced it, inhaling rapidly and evenly. She closed her eyes, her brow in wrinkles as she grimaced with pain. He stood, powerless, watching the hand within her clenching itself tightly, until her face was one that he had never seen before, a screwed-up mask of desperation which suddenly and slowly relaxed, wrinkles fading, eyes opening, as the contraction subsided.

She looked up at him and smiled. "He must have turned around last week. Remember the bump we felt high on my stomach? That was his head."

"We'll be swinging him down the road soon," said Laski.

Her smile suddenly disappeared as the next contraction came. She went into her rapid breathing and he willed her his strength, trying to make it pass out of his body and enter hers.

The nurse came in as the contraction subsided. "How're we doing?"

"All right."

"Let me have a look." The nurse lifted Diane's gown for a moment, then lowered it. "You're dilating beautifully."

Diane's smile was once again ruined by the return of a contraction.

A young intern entered and stood at the foot of the bed, waiting as the contraction worked toward its peak. He looked at Laski and asked politely, "Would you mind stepping outside a moment while we examine her?"

Laski went out into the hallway. What do they do to her that I can't be there? Does he think I've never seen my wife's body before? Don't send bad vibrations. They're running this show. He walked up and down the hallway, feeling like the odd man out.

The door opened; the intern came into the hallway and nodded at Laski, who went back in and joined the nurse at the foot of the bed.

"You're fully dilated," said the nurse to Diane. "You can start pushing anytime you want."

Diane nodded her head as the next contraction hit. Laski went behind her, lifting her up from the back, as they had practiced. He lifted and she hauled back on her knees with her hands, bending her legs and spreading them apart, pressing down within herself. He held her up for the length of the contraction and then slowly let her down.

"Very nice," said the nurse. "Keep up the good work." She smiled at them and left the room.

"Would you wet a washcloth and put it on my forehead?"

Laski got a washcloth out of her bag and wet it in the bathroom sink. He wiped her brow, her cheeks, her neck. "Where's the doctor?"

"He's sleeping in a room down the hall. They'll wake him up when it's time."

"How do you feel?"

"I'm glad to be pushing."

The contraction came and he lifted her again, his face close to hers. The wrinkled brow and tight-closed eyes formed a face he'd never dreamed of. All her beauty was gone, and she seemed like a sexless creature struggling for all it was worth, laboring greatly with the beginning of the world. Their laughter, their little joys, their plans, everything they'd known was swallowed by this labor, a work he suddenly wished they'd never begun, so contorted was she, so unlike the woman he knew. Her face was red, her temples pounding, and she looked now like a middle-aged man taking a shit that was killing him. This is humanity, thought Laski, and he questioned the purpose of a race that seeks to perpetuate itself in agony, but before he had his answer, the contraction had passed and he was lowering her back to the pillow.

He took the washcloth, wet it again and wiped her perspiring face. "Relax deeply now. Get your energy back. Spread your legs—relax your arms." He talked softly, smoothing out her still-trembling limbs until she finally lay quiet, eyes closed.

The wave came again and carried them out onto the sea of pain, where he wondered again why life ever came into the world. The loveliness of the highway night, when all the stars seemed watching, was now drowned in sweat. The most beautiful face he'd ever seen was looking bulbous, red, and homely.

The tide that drew them out into the troubled waters once again spent itself and they floated slowly back, resting for a minute or so, only to be dragged out again. He held her up while she contracted and pushed inside herself, trying to open the petals of her flowering body. He'd thought that such a miraculous opening would somehow be performed in a more splendid fashion. But she was sweating like a lumberjack's horse after a summer morning of hauling logs.

He lifted her, trying to free the load she was struggling with, but she was straining against the traces, getting nowhere, her eyes like those of a draft horse—puzzled, frustrated, and enslaved. He could see the strain pulsing in her reddened temples, just as he'd seen it in the workhorses when he thought they would surely die of a heart attack, racing as they did through the woods with huge logs behind them, jamming suddenly on a stump, the reins almost snapping and their mighty muscles knotting against the obstacle. Who would choose this, thought Laski, this work, this woe? Life enslaves us,

makes us want children, gives us a thousand illu-
sions about love, and all so that it can go forward.

He felt the supremacy of life, its power greater
than his will. I just wanted to be with you, Diane,
the two of us living easily together and here we are,
with your life on the line.

She was coming down the staircase of a brownstone
building. She wore a long purple cape with a high collar
turned up around her neck. The cape flared out as she
touched the sidewalk and he stood rooted and stupid,
struggling to speak. She must have felt it, for she turned
and looked his way.

Her face contracted again, her eyes closing
tightly and her mouth bending into a mask formed
by the pain that came on her again. He held her up,
feeling the strain in her muscles and the fever in her
skin. The short ringlets of hair at her neck were
soaked and glistening. A wet spot was spreading
across her back.

THE INTERN AND the nurse returned while they were out upon the waves, struggling together, pushing together, sweating together to bring the thing to completion, and when the contraction ended the intern did not ask Laski to leave while he made his examination. "You're showing some progress now."

"You can see the baby," said the nurse.

Laski looked down, and in the shaved and sweating crack he saw something pink and strange, a little patch of flesh he could not comprehend. All he knew were the waves that took them out again, where they were alone in love and sadness that none else could share, alone and clinging to each other in the reality they had long prepared for, for which no preparation was ever enough.

"I've seen you before," he said, *stopping her on Broadway.*

"Have you?" she said, *the slightest touch of flirtation in her voice, just enough to keep him coming toward her, out of his deep embarrassed nature.*

Back they drifted, to the green room in the sleeping hospital.

Hardly had they rested when the waves carried them out again, like a nightmare that repeats itself over and over through the night, and over and over again through the years. Back and forth they went and he feared that her strength could not hold. He had no confidence, not in himself, nor in her. He felt like a helpless child, and Diane seemed helpless too, their long struggle getting them nowhere, only repeating itself—contraction, release, contraction again. But the nurse and intern seemed unconcerned by it all, were cheerful and confident. And the doctor is down the hall, sleeping. He's not worried. If there were anything wrong he'd be here.

She dressed by the window of his tiny room, slipping slowly into tight knit slacks and sweater. Her short hair needed no combing or fixing, and she was the most natural thing he'd ever seen, unlike his previous loves, who'd always thrown him out of the room while they dressed and primped or put curlers in their hair.

Her gown was wringing wet, her hair plastered down, as if the sea had broken over her. She closed her eyes and crow's-feet came there, lines he'd never seen before, lines of age, and he knew that ages had passed. "Again," she said, her voice almost a sob now, but not a sob, too tired for tears. And he lifted her up as the tide carried them out again, into the wild uncharted waters.

He held her, his love for her expanding with every tremor of her body. It seemed he'd never loved her before, that all of their past was just a rehearsal for this moment in which he felt resounding inside him all the days of her life, days before he'd known her, days from the frightened child's face he saw

before him, and days from the wise woman's an-
cient life that came calling now to give her unknown
strength. All the frustration of Diane's thirty years
was present, and she seemed to be making a wish
in the well of time, that everything should finally
come out all right, that finally something she was
doing would be just as it should be.

"I can't have a baby," she said, "because of the shape
of my womb."

"Bullshit."

"He's a Park Avenue gynecologist."

Well, thought Laski, it took us ten years but we
finally made one. He lowered her back to the bed,
wiping her brow with the washcloth. She smiled,
but it again was a mask, formed by momentary release from her anguish. In it was none of the flirtation, none of the peace, none of the things he
usually saw in her smiles. But he knew she'd made
this smile for him, to ease his worry. She's seeing
into me too; maybe she sees all the care of my days,
as I am seeing her. He felt them together, then, on
a new level, older, wiser, with pain as the binder in

their union. We came more than fifty miles tonight; we've crossed the ocean.

Her smile suddenly drew itself up beyond the limits of smiling, becoming a grimace, and he lifted her up. We're not across the ocean yet.

"Gee-yup, Bob!" The great horse pulled, his hooves scraping on the forest floor, sending moss and sticks flying. The tree creaked and swayed and fell and Bob-horse ran with it, dragging branches and all.

"I guess we can get Doctor Barker now," said the intern.

The nurse went out of the room. Laski wiped Diane's brow and the intern stood at the foot of the bed, watching. "You've been pushing for nearly three hours," he said.

"That's too long, isn't it?" she asked.

"It's because the baby's weight is up instead of down."

And suddenly they were out again, in the tempest. Laski held her up, pouring himself through his fingertips into her, as she lifted her legs and pushed.

The nurse entered with a tall young man in

white uniform. He stood at the foot of the bed with the intern as Laski and Diane held on, out upon the sea, love-blown sailors lost in fathomless depths of time and destiny, coming now slowly back to a room of strangers who seemed eternal too, in a never-ending play. "If you'll just step outside a minute," said Doctor Barker.

Laski went into the hallway and gathered himself together in a single prayer without words, offered to the ocean.

The door swung open. The young doctor stepped out and said, "Things are developing now. We'll be taking her down to the delivery room."

Laski went back to Diane. She was bent up, contracting alone, and he went to her.

"Your baby's on the way now," said the nurse, smiling cheerfully at Laski.

He suddenly remembered the baby, the little swimmer in the secret sea. He's struggling too, struggling to be with us, struggling just like we are.

Laski's heart became an ocean of love, as nine months of memories flooded him, and the baby was real again, real as in the night when Laski felt tiny feet kicking inside Diane. Our baby, our little friend, is being born!

And this, thought Laski, is why we labor, so that love might come into the world.

THE CONTRACTION PASSED, and he and Diane were washed back, limp like sea-plants when the waves abandon them on the shore. "It looks very good," said the intern.

The nurse came in, wheeling a stretcher. "All set?"

"Yes," said Diane. They slid her from the bed onto the stretcher and they all walked beside it down the hallway toward the delivery room. Doctor Barker was being put into a white gown. Laski leaned over and kissed Diane.

"Aren't you coming in?" she asked, her voice filled with longing.

The nurse continued wheeling her into the delivery room and Laski stood in the hall outside. His will, his speech, his guts were gone. Barker stepped over to him. "The nurse will give you a cap and gown and you can watch from behind the table."

Laski's strength came back in a whirlwind as a great smile crossed his face. We're going all the way together! He stood, watching the doctor and intern wash their hands in a nearby sink, washing them again and again, in slow methodical manner. The nurse came to him and held up a gown. He slipped his arms into it and she tied it in back. She gave him a white cap which he fastened over his ears. Then he and the intern went into the delivery room, where Diane lay on the central table, her legs in stirrups, her wrists strapped down.

"You can sit here," said the nurse, setting a stool behind the table. Another nurse fixed the mirror that was above the table, so that Laski could see the area of birth.

"A clear picture?"

"Perfect."

One of the nurses then brought a little sponge soaked with surgical soap, and wiped Diane's vaginal area.

"Oh, that feels good."

"Has she had any anesthetic?" asked the other nurse.

"No."

"Well, now, isn't she wonderful?"

Doctor Barker came and sat on a stool at the other end of the table. "I'm going to drain your bladder."

He inserted a tube into her urethra and a moment later her urine ran out of it, into a bucket at Barker's feet.

"I have a contraction," said Diane.

"Go ahead and push."

Laski could not reach her, and she lifted herself, working alone. When the contraction subsided, Barker said, "I'm going to make a small cut. First I'll give you something to numb it." He inserted a needle at the edge of her vagina, making three injections. Then he pinched her skin with a tweezers.

"Do you feel that?"

"No."

He made an incision, cutting sideways toward her thigh. "Check the heartbeat."

The nurse laid her stethoscope on Diane's lower belly and listened, timing the baby's heartbeat with her watch.

"Normal."

"All right—push again." Barker inserted his finger into Diane's vagina, feeling for the baby. When the finger came out, Laski saw more of the strange pink skin, and a thick dark substance.

"Don't let that worry you," said the nurse to Laski. "The baby's just had a bowel movement."

"Push," said Barker. Diane pushed and Laski could see the baby's rear end, at the doorway of the world, ass-backwards, thought Laski, but coming!

"All right, dear, push again," said Barker.

She pushed and he put his long fingers into her vagina, moving them around and spreading her lips. Suddenly a foot appeared, followed by a long limp leg. Barker quickly brought the other leg down and

Laski looked at it in wonder, at the tiny toenails and the perfectly formed little feet that had been developing all along within her, about which he had dreamed so often, envisioning them in countless ways, and now the first step of those little feet into life had come before his eyes.

"It's a boy!" exclaimed the nurse.

Laski's heart filled with joy. Staring at the entranceway, he saw the tiny penis and a second later it squirted a jet of urine.

"I felt him pee on me!" cried Diane in wonder.

"Push," said Barker. "Push with all you've got."

As she pushed he guided the tiny body out, all but the head, which remained inside. Laski stared in fascination at the dangling little creature, the skin gray and wet—his little son, come at last.

Barker inserted the forceps. "Once again."

Diane pushed and Laski tensed as he watched Barker forcefully pulling with the forceps to release the head. My God, thought Laski, they handle them hard. And suddenly the head popped out and the child was free.

Barker's hands moved with incredible grace and swiftness, turning the baby in the air, holding him up like a red rose. Laski saw a face filled with rage, yet triumphant, the god of time and men, whose closed eyes looked straight into Laski's and said, *See, see, this!*

"Cut the cord!"

The intern severed the cord and Barker carried the child with utmost delicacy in his two hands, moving quickly over to a table by the wall.

"The aspirator," he said, sharply.

The nurse handed him an instrument that looked like an old car horn, a rubber bulb fitted on the end of it. He put it to the baby's face and squeezed.

The child lay perfectly still. Barker worked the pump, then touched the limp wrist, lifting it for a moment and laying it back down. One nurse massaged the feet, and the other handed Barker a length of fine hose which he inserted into the baby's mouth. He breathed into it, and Laski watched his son's chest rise and fall with the breath of the doctor moving inside him.

Barker stopped for a moment, wiped his brow, returned to the blowing-tube. Laski looked on, watching the lungs rise and fall again. The rest of the body lay perfectly still. How long his legs are, thought Laski— just like his mother's.

Barker removed the tube and put his mouth to the child's, blowing into it with his lips pressed against the tiny mouth.

The nurse continued to massage the feet. Laski looked at the clock on the wall: Four-thirty-five.

Barker stepped back, wiped his brow again, and Laski remembered moments from his own life, when he'd worked on things, and found them puzzling, and unyielding, and he'd wiped his brow that way. Barker put the aspirator back on the still little body, and pumped it, a little sighing noise coming from the rubber bulb.

"Is that the baby?" asked Diane.

Laski looked at her, and looked away, drawn back to his little son, to the little arm that rose and fell so limply in Barker's hand.

"Where's the baby?" asked Diane.

"He's over there," said Laski softly.

Barker removed the aspirator and put his mouth to the child's again, blowing in and out, gently, evenly. He stepped back, wiped his brow, turned to Laski, and shook his head from side to side.

Laski nodded.

It was over.

He turned and sat down on the little stool beside the table. The intern was stitching Diane's opened vagina.

"Does that hurt?"

"No," she said, laughing nervously.

Laski looked at her flat stomach. How can she possibly hold together in the face of this? How do we tell her?

He turned to the table by the wall. The baby had been lowered into a glass case and he was on his side, eyes closed. Laski saw resignation in the little face, the expression of work completely done, like a man who has rolled over to sleep at the end of the day.

"Are you all right?" asked Barker.

"Yes," said Laski.

Barker stepped over to the maternity table and looked down at Diane.

She raised her eyes to his. "I know," she said.

"I'm sorry."

"It's not your fault," she said, a sob breaking from her throat.

"The baby looks perfectly normal," said Barker. "There's no reason why you can't have another child."

Laski listened numbly. He thinks that's what has been at stake, our wish for a child, any child, not this particular child who swung down the road between us. They can't know how special he is. They point to the future. But we're here, forever, now.

The nurse slipped Diane onto the wheeled table. "I have a needle for you," said the nurse.

"No," said Diane, still refusing any anesthetic.

"It's to dry up your milk," said the nurse, gently.

"There are no private rooms," said the other nurse. "We can put you in a semiprivate."

"I can go to a ward," said Diane. "I only wanted a private room so I could keep the baby with me."

"It would be better for you in a semiprivate. All the other babies will be brought into the ward for feeding, and they'll make you feel bad."

"I wouldn't mind the babies," said Diane, crying softly. "But I'd probably make all the other mothers feel bad."

They wheeled her through the dimly lit hallway and Laski walked beside her, to a room with two beds, both of them empty. They helped her into the bed and drew the covers over her.

"May I stay?" asked Laski.

"Yes, certainly," said the nurse. "Do you want to sleep on the other bed?"

"No, I'm not tired."

"If you want to," she said, "just flop down on it." The nurse leaned over to Diane. "These things happen. I'm sure you'll have better luck next time."

Laski looked at the little handbag beside the bed, in which Diane had packed two baby washcloths, one pink, one blue, and he saw that it was the blue one he'd been using to mop her brow.

She looked quietly at him, and stroked his hair with her hand. He laid his head down on the bed beside her, as the full weight of his own weariness took him. The nurse came in again and said, "Are you sure you won't lie down?"

"All right," he said, and walked over to the other bed.

"Let me slip this sheet over it. I'm lazy. I don't want to have to make it again."

He crawled onto the top sheet and lay looking at the ceiling. Beneath his head he felt cement blocks. He drifted, into kaleidoscopic sleep, so filled with images he could not sort them into any recognizable dream, and they rushed over him like water.

He woke and saw Diane looking at the ceiling. He got up and sat beside her again. The dawn was breaking. Through the window he saw another wing of the hospital, and beyond that the street, on which the gray light was falling. He watched the street as the sunlight fell upon it.

In the hallway the sound of dishes began. "They're bringing breakfast," she said.

The breakfast carts came closer, and an elderly woman entered, carrying a tray. She smiled at Laski. "Well, it's a lovely day, isn't it?"

Diane ate cereal and toast, and sunlight found the room.

"They'll want me out of here soon," said Laski.

"Yes, the mothers will be feeding their babies."

He saw the sorrow break over her for a moment, like a wave upon a cliff, but the wave washed away, and there was the cliff, which sorrow could not drown.

"I'll be back this evening," he said. "Visiting hours are at seven. Is there anything you want?"

"No, just you."

He leaned over and kissed her, her tears going slowly down his cheek.

Laski drove over the bridge and out of town. As he crossed the railroad tracks that ran through the slum on the edge of the city, a delicate film of light came across his eyes, as if a shimmering translucent veil were covering the morning, and he knew that it was his son's spirit, riding with him. And then he saw himself running with his son, through the fields, leaping the old broken fences. They walked to the stream and dove into it, then danced upon it, then ran to the trees, climbing up above the mist.

Laski drove toward home with tears streaming down his face, his spirit racing with his son through time, across the morning of the world, from place to place, in cities and in the lovely valley. The moment of their meeting was endless: they took a boat, and took a train, and saw the sights, and grew up together. It seemed to take years getting to the forest, and as Laski climbed the hills into the abandoned settlement, he felt the spirit of his son spreading out all around him. Spreading out as it did, into every tree and cloud, he felt it losing personality, felt it dissolving into something remote, expanded beyond his powers to follow. He's going now, thought Laski. He's grown-up and leaving me. Good-bye, good-bye, he called, looking out to the beautiful eastern sky where the sun was dazzling the trees.

You're free in the wind. You're great with the winds and sun.

Then it was over and Laski was alone again, bouncing along the old winding road through the forest.

Returning to the hospital in the evening, he got lost in the corridors beyond the lobby, none of it familiar to him anymore. He stood looking toward a staircase he could not remember climbing before. A strong voice came at his shoulder. "Where are you headed for?"

"Maternity."

"Follow me," said a powerfully striding man in boots and ski sweater. He took the steps as if they were a mountain trail and Laski kept the pace.

"What did you have?" asked the man, not looking back, keeping his eyes on the trail.

Laski hesitated as fragments of explanations rose in his mind—*the baby died, we had nothing*—but then he felt the spirit of the child again, suddenly surging in his heart, and he said, "A boy."

"Congratulations," said the mountain-man, as they reached the top of the mountain staircase, at the hall marked MATERNITY.

"And you?" asked Laski.

"A boy," said the mountaineer, his voice filled with wind and stone and wild joy. He turned off to the left, and Laski went straight ahead, down the hall to Diane's room.

She was in bed, her eyes red, her face pale, the shock of the night still on her. He sat down beside the bed and took her hand. "Was the doctor in to see you?"

"He said he examined the afterbirth and found that the cord had been connected to the edge of the placenta instead of the middle. It was a weak place and at the last minute the cord tore. The baby bled."

Laski slowly nodded his head and looked toward the window. Through the other lighted rooms of the hospital he saw distant figures moving.

"He'd like to perform an autopsy," said Diane.

"Is it really necessary?"

"It's up to us."

"Do you want to let them?"

"I guess they always do it."

Beyond the windows of the hospital, he could see the sidewalks and the snowy street. In the maternity hallway, at the desk, the nurses were chatting and laughing together.

"He's in the morgue," said Diane.

A nurse entered the room, smiling cheerfully. "Time for your heat lamp." Then, turning to Laski, "Would you excuse us for a minute?"

Laski stepped out into the hall. The doors of the other rooms were open and he could see women in their beds, visitors beside them. He lowered his eyes toward the floor and followed the sound of the waxing machine and the elevator and the visiting voices, all of it flowing like a stream in which he seemed to be floating. The second hand on the wall clock over his head was humming, round and round.

The laughter at the nurse's desk continued, and he realized it was New Year's Eve. *In a room on 91st Street in New York City, in the darkness of a little bed, while the bells rang and the sirens called, he held her.* The waxing machine appeared, its long whiskers whirring around and around over the tiled floor.

A SNOWSTORM HAD begun in the city. The night was cold, and he was filled with tired thoughts. Twenty-five miles away, out in the woods, the house was waiting, empty and cold. A hotel would be warm and bright—a single room, a table with a lamp on it, a bed. I could get some sleep and hang around town tomorrow until visiting time.

The traffic light turned green through the veil of falling snow, and he drove down the main street of town to the street of the hotel, where he parked the truck. The snow was coming harder. He walked along toward the hotel. It's not the best and that's all I need, just a flop for the night.

His body ached and his eyes were tired. The shops on the street were all closed, the merchandise on display beneath dim nightlights, and he passed by it all on weary legs. The hotel had a single door leading to a cramped little lobby, into which he stepped, looking toward the night clerk's desk. The clerk, reading a newspaper, did not look up. A television set was going, and two men sat before it, smiling at some flickering image Laski could not see, but he sensed the loneliness of the men, and their desperate fight against it, huddled together before the television.

As if turned by a magnet, he went back out through the door into the street. The snow fell on him as he walked back to the truck and climbed into it, driving out of town and over the white highway toward the woods.

HE ENTERED THE cabin reluctantly, as if it were a cave of ghosts. The stove was low and he stirred it up. When the surface was hot, he slid on a frying pan and cooked himself supper. He ate slowly, staring out the window at the whirling snow. When his meal was finished, he washed the dishes, not hurrying, but working slowly, with concentration, leaving no room for morbid thoughts, ghosts, fears. There was only the hot water, the dish, his hands, the soapy rag.

The stairs to the second floor looked dark and foreboding, and what's up there, amidst the baby clothes and crib? There's nothing up there, he said, and he walked up the stairs and undressed in the small bedroom. He kept the light on for a few minutes and then, resigning himself to darkness and sleep, switched it off.

Alone in the dark house far out in the woods, with a storm blowing on the outside and the shadow of death on the inside, he crawled beneath the covers. Spectres rose up behind his closed eyes, weird and menacing. He watched his mind play out its age-old fears, and trembling, he fell into dreams, finding himself outside the cabin, walking through the dream-forest. Beside a tree he saw a cloaked and hooded figure. The figure turned and the face beneath the hood was a smiling skull of stone. Death held out his walking stick, and Laski took it in his hand.

LATE AFTERNOON SUNLIGHT streamed through the hospital window and he sat down beside her again. She looked stronger, and the storm was over.

"We have to bury the baby," she said. "They don't want him in the morgue anymore."

"We can bury him in the woods."

"That's what I told the nurse. She said it was highly unusual, but that it would probably be all right. She had a lot of forms. We'll have to have a witness."

"How about the autopsy? Won't the baby be…?"

"She said they put him back together again."

Doctor Barker came into the room. They both looked at him in silence. He stood, tall and uncomfortable at the foot of the bed. "The autopsy showed your baby was perfectly normal. There's no reason why what happened should ever happen again."

"Do you think she can go home tomorrow?"

"How do your stitches feel?"

"They burn a little, that's all."

"I suppose you can leave, if you'll feel better at home." He turned to go, then turned back to Diane. "I know it's difficult to lose your first baby when you're thirty."

THE LAST LIGHT of day went along the brick wall of the hospital. Laski sat by the window, watching as night came on. Diane, wearing a bathrobe, entered the room. "I told the nurse we'd be taking the baby home tomorrow afternoon."

"I'll build a little box for him tonight."

"Will you be able to dig a hole in the frozen ground?"

A nurse peeked her head inside the door. "There are some fluids in the hall if either of you want any."

Laski went out and found a tray of watered fruit drinks. He poured some orange into two glasses and returned to the room. "Fluids," he said, handing her the thin orange drink.

The night visiting bell sounded. "I'll be in first thing tomorrow afternoon," he said, kissing her lightly on the lips. Then he went down the green hall, toward the street, the highway, and home.

THE STEEL ROOF of the cabin was bright in the moonlight as he parked the truck in the drive. He opened the door to the shed, where his lumber was piled. How am I going to do this? he asked himself, looking at the long pile of pine boards, and at his tools. He was overcome by a feeling of dread about making the coffin; he had no wish to build it, or anything, ever again.

He fingered the smoothly planed surface of the boards; the heavy feeling in him remained, as if he were in a dark cloud, but he grabbed a board and hauled it out of the pile.

Carrying the sawhorses into his studio, he spaced them out evenly. Across them he laid the long clean pine board. Then he brought his toolbox in and set it down. He pulled the metallic rule out of its case and stretched it along the wood, imagining the size of the baby's body.

He laid his T-square on the mark, drew a straight line and sawed along it, thinking of the old days when men had always built the caskets of their loved ones, and he saw that it was a good thing to do, that it was a privilege few men had anymore. He marked the next line carefully and sawed a matching piece to form the floor of the casket.

He joined the two pieces and then cut the sides and ends for the box. The time passed slowly and peacefully. He worked, sanding the edges of the pieces so that they would join well, to form a box that no one would see, but which had to be made perfectly. He drilled holes and countersunk them, and screwed on the sides and endpieces.

Squatting on the floor, sawdust on his knees and a pencil behind his ear, he turned the screws slowly, biting deep into the wood. He sanded along the edge of the box, making another fine cloud of sawdust, which filled his nose with a memorable smell. I built a house for us, with a room for him, and now I'm building his casket. There's no difference in the work. We simply must go along, eyes open, watching our work carefully, without any extra thoughts. Then we flow with the night.

The little box took shape and he resisted feeling proud of it, for pride was something extra. I do it quietly, for no one, not even for him, for he's gone beyond my little box. But he left behind a fragment of himself, which requires a box I can carry through the woods. And the box needs a lid and I've got to find a pair of hinges.

He rummaged around the shed and found an old rusted pair, small and squeaky, but serviceable. Making the outlines for the hinges, he chiseled out their shape, so they slid snugly down into the wood. He tried the lid and continued setting the hinges, until the lid finally closed solidly. He worked the lid up and down a few times, enjoying the smooth action of it, until he remembered what it was for, and he saw again that there should be nothing extra in the work.

He put away the sawhorses and his tools, and swept up the dust. Then he sat down in a chair and quietly rocked, back and forth, looking at the coffin. A vague dissatisfaction stirred in him, growing slowly more clear and troubling.

If we bury him here, we'll be attached to this land permanently. I can have him cremated at a funeral home, and his ashes will be put in a little metal box and we can carry it around with us when we travel. And when we get to the middle of the ocean someday, we can throw his ashes there.

That's exactly what we should do. I'll take him to the funeral home tomorrow and they can cremate him in the little coffin.

A feeling of freedom came to Laski—freedom from land and houses and graves. And keeping this thought in his mind, he went upstairs to bed.

WHEN HE ENTERED the hospital room, it was into a new atmosphere—the other bed was now occupied. As he went toward Diane, out of the corner of his eye he saw a young girl lying in the bed he had lain in. Beside her was a young man, and two older women. They pulled a curtain around themselves, and Laski sat down beside Diane.

"She lost her baby," whispered Diane.

Laski glanced toward the closed curtain, behind which soft shadows were moving. "I think we should have the baby cremated in town this afternoon."

"But why?"

"If we bury him on the land, it will just be another tie for us, that this is the place where the baby
is buried."

Her eyes filled with tears again. "If you think
it's best...."

"I don't know what's best," he said. "Maybe
there isn't any best. But the thought was very strong
and I'm trying to flow with it."

"What will you do?"

"I'll go over to the funeral home now and find
out if they can do it right away."

He stood and went past the other visitors.
Down the hall once more, and down the stairs, his
thoughts were racing now—to get it over with, and
set them free.

He crossed the parking lot quickly and started
the truck. Vaguely remembering the whereabouts
of a funeral home, he drove through town. They'll
deal with the whole thing, and we won't have to get
involved.

Snowplows were still working, clearing the
streets, and here and there people were shoveling

out their sidewalks and driveways. Laski turned a corner and saw the old colonial manor with the black and white nameplate on one of its large old pillars. It was an enormous place, with many windows, and he looked through the front window, down a long hallway lined with flowers and muted floor lamps. The parking lot was filled with cars. Three large limousines were heaped with flowers, and a crew of professionally somber men in black were standing beside a fourth limousine, hung with gray velvet curtains. The side door opened and the front end of a casket came out, made of dark wood polished to a high gloss and trimmed with silver and gold filigree. Clinging to its shining brass carrying-rails was a crew of professionals, waxed-faced and silent, bearing the huge gaudy coffin toward the hearse, where the back door was opened smoothly by a driver, who helped to slide the coffin into the richly curtained interior.

Laski drove on, horrified. What in hell did I almost do?

His hands were trembling on the wheel. Tears in his eyes, he looked down at the little pine box on the seat beside him, and laid his hand upon its plain smooth surface.

Circling back through town, he returned to the hospital; once again through the corridors, once again up the stairs, once again past the nurses, and past the people visiting in Diane's room.

"Let's go," he said softly, taking Diane's hand. "We're going home together, and we'll bury him down by the stream."

"But what about the funeral home?"

"Just something I dreamed up to protect myself from the truth of death."

She got up from the bed. "I just have to get dressed," she said, taking her clothes into the bathroom; he sat on the edge of the bed, and heard the voices of the visitors talking to the young girl behind the curtain.

"You mustn't think about it anymore."

"Tomorrow's another day."

"Yes," said the girl. And then again, *"Yes,"* softly.

"That's right, dear. You should always look to the future."

"What a pretty nightgown."

"I got it at the K-Mart."

"They'll have the sales there now."

"Everything will be half-price. After New Year's."

Smoke drifted over the curtain. Laski went to the window. The previous day's paper was on the windowsill, and glancing at the headlines he saw war, scandal, inflation. We'll bury him by the stream. This moment dies and is followed by another moment which also dies. Moment to moment I go.

"I'm ready," she said. He picked up her bag and they went to the desk. An elderly nurse spoke to them. "I've told them to have the baby ready for you down at the reception desk. He'll be all wrapped nicely."

Another nurse appeared with a wheelchair.

"I can walk," said Diane.

"Rules," said the nurse. "You get to ride."

Diane sat in the chair and they went to the elevator. The nurse wheeled her into it and Laski stood beside her as they rode down to the lobby.

The usual crowd was there, reading magazines and staring at the pale yellow walls. The nurse wheeled them to the reception room. "The Laski baby," she said.

The receptionist went into the room behind her and returned with an orderly, who carried a small linen bundle.

Diane, still in the wheelchair, held her arms out, a sob breaking in her throat. The orderly stood puzzled, not knowing what to do.

Laski reached out and took the cold little parcel, cradling it in one arm, and carrying Diane's suitcase with the other. They went up the exit ramp toward the door. He looked down at Diane and saw her still crying.

"I'll bring the truck to the door," he said, and went out across the parking lot, with the baby still in his arms. He could not feel the outline of the body, only the small weight of it in the cold linen wrapping. From a refrigerator, he thought, and then he opened the truck and slid inside.

With the baby on his lap, he opened the pine

box and laid the linen-shrouded child into it. He closed the lid and latched it shut. The nurse was waiting at the sidewalk as he drove up to the entrance of the hospital. They helped Diane out of the chair and into the front seat of the truck "You'll have better luck next time," said the nurse. She waved to them, standing for a moment beneath the hospital awning, and then as they pulled away she turned with the empty wheelchair.

"It's a lovely box," said Diane, her voice calm now.

The box was between them on the seat, and for a moment Laski smelled the sweet perfume of death, or was it the smell of the wood? The delicate odor continued to come to him as they went along the highway, by the fields and the river. The day was unseasonably warm, with wisps of gray mist above the water, and the snow was changing to slush along the shoulder of the road.

"It's just us again," he said.

"Yes," she said, their hands touching on the lid of the pine box.

He wheeled the truck up into the wooded hills, along the old road toward their home. Above an abandoned farm a crow went through the January sky, black wings beating slowly on the gray heights.

Laski turned down the lane to the cabin, and into the drive. He got out and opened the door for her. She stepped into the snow, leaning on him. The sound of melting snow as it dripped off the trees filled the air, and the smell of the trees came strong on the moist warm breeze.

"What a beautiful day," she said, suddenly crying again.

He walked with her slowly up the shoveled path to their door. She leaned on him into the cabin; he had the couch made up for her and settled her onto it. Then he stirred the fire and went back out to the car for her bag, and then back again, for the pine box.

He placed the box down on top of the table, and it remained there in the last light of the afternoon, while they sat quietly on the couch.

"I'd better go see old Ben and ask him to come here in the morning." Laski went out again and he saw her watching him through the window.

Ben's collie dog came bounding up to Laski's truck, and Laski got out and petted him, rolling him over on his back and scratching his stomach. He knelt in the snow for a moment, his hand on the dog's belly. In the sky the crow was still calling, circling on the wind, and Laski felt as if he were the crow and the dog and the sky, as if he were transparent and the day was passing through him.

"Come into my castle, friend."

Laski looked up and saw old Ben standing in the doorway of the broken-down farmhouse. Ben led him through the labyrinth of boards and falling rafters, into the innermost room of the house, where an old iron stove was glowing with heat and everything was neatly in place—table, chair, water bucket, and a small single bed behind the stove. The hermit sat down on the edge of the bed and tossed a chunk of wood into the fire. "Well, what can we do for you today?" he asked, taking out a package of tobacco.

Laski hesitated, holding his hands out over the heated top of the stove. "The baby died," he said.

Ben stared at the cracked old firebox of the stove, where tiny sparks were dancing.

"Will you help me bury him?" asked Laski.

"You'll have to get a lot number from the cemetery," said the hermit, trying to roll a cigarette, the tobacco sticking out at both ends.

"I'm burying him in the woods."

Ben hesitated, looking at Laski across the stove. "Do you have a permit?"

"It's OK, Ben. They filled out the papers at the hospital. I put your name in as the witness." He stared back down at the stove. How scared we are, he thought, to even bury our dead, unless we have permission from the government. "I'd like to do it first thing in the morning."

"I'll be there," said Ben.

Laski went back through the winding tunnel of debris and out into the snow. The dog jumped up to him, licking his hand, and Laski saw all the sad wisdom of dogs flickering in the collie's dark eyes.

THE SUN WAS gone, and they sat quietly, looking toward the box. Finally she said, "I'd like to see him."

"All right," said Laski, his stomach going weak. He had a fleeting image in his mind of the baby he had seen, a powerful face looking at him in the moment of death. What will he look like now, thought Laski, dreading the opening of the box.

He slowly lifted the lid and touched the linen bundle. It was still cool. He felt as though he were in a dream again. "You'd better let me look at him first, in case he's too badly marked." He turned back the clean crisp linen. Beneath it was a faded, dirty

piece of sheet, its edges torn and frayed. He unfolded it, expecting to suddenly see the little face,
but beneath the sheet were old pieces of rags laid on
top of each other, and beneath the old rags was a
green plastic garbage bag.

He untwisted the piece of wire that held the
garbage bag closed. Slowly pulling down the edge of
the bag, he came to the proud little head, now gray
and cold. Gently, he rolled down the rest of the
garbage bag and looked into the open cavity of his
son's chest and stomach.

"They left him open," he said, his hands trembling on the bag.

"It's all right," she said. "I saw."

Laski unfolded the garbage bag until the baby
was completely visible, his torso a hollow of skin
right to the backbone, holding a little pool of blood,
like a cup. Drifting in the blood was a plastic stick
with a number on it.

A fire raged through Laski's body, swelling his
chest with blood and burning his throat. "This is
death!" he cried, tears bursting from his eyes.

"There's nothing strange about it!"

He moved his eyes down the long legs where the little feet were tucked together, one atop the other, and death was upon them, holding them still as stone. He looked again into the open hole in the baby's body, to the framework of the backbone. They took out his lungs and his stomach, took out all his guts. They even took his little heart.

Laski was engulfed again by love for the little boy who lay before him, all cut-up. He took the right hand in his own, opening the stiff little fingers and gazing into the tiny cold palm. The fingers held firm against his, with death's unbending grip. How tiny his fingernails are, and so perfect.

He looked at the face of his son and saw that it had undergone a strange transformation. The features had completely matured, the face now that of a man of many years, as if the single moment of life when he was spun upon the doctor's hand had been a lifetime from beginning to end. The triumph and rage, the gain and loss, all this was gone from the face now, and the closed eyelids radiated serenity.

"He's so lovely," said Diane, her tears falling on the exquisite little head, finely sculpted as that of a Grecian statue. "He struggled so hard to be born...."

Then the ocean of sorrow took her and she was crying wildly, like a seawind that drives the water into terrible waves. And through the storm the little pine box floated calmly, with its strange passenger, the infant who was also an old man.

Laski open the little eyelid and saw a blackened jewel, gone far into the night. He closed it and put his mouth to the little ear, into which he whispered, "Don't be afraid." Then, looking at the high broad forehead and the noble eyelids, and seeing again so clearly the wisdom they embodied, he knew the being who had come to them and left so quickly didn't need any advice. And he felt much younger than this infant who lay before him, this infant with the head of an age-old sage.

"He never got to live at all!" cried Diane, howling in the seawind.

Laski touched the little cheek and it sagged beneath his touch, the lifeless flesh like softest putty.

"Oh no, don't," said Diane, her voice suddenly soft, as she gently pushed the flesh of the cheek back into place. Bending her head over, she laid a kiss upon the little forehead. "He's just like marble."

Laski slowly brought the garbage bag up around the little body.

"I could look at him forever," said Diane, but she wrapped the bag in the old rags and the dirty sheet, finally pinning closed the clean white linen. Laski lowered the lid of the box, and again it seemed like a dream that could move in any direction he willed. But then he felt reality moving in only one direction. The baby was born and he died and I'm closing the lid of his coffin.

Diane wiped the baby's blood from Laski's face and from her own lips, then went slowly to the couch and lay down. He sat on the floor beside her. There was nothing to say. Neither of them wished to escape the passing of the hours, and they were powerless to change the winding stream of the night; there was nothing to do but sit in the stillness.

He fell into reverie and he fell into fantasy. He was back in the labor room, seeing the baby's skin pushing at her vagina. *He's right there—he's waiting. Get him out of there—don't waste any more time.* But the doctor slept down the hall.

Finally his thoughts faded and there was only the sound of the winter night outside. He felt Diane with him in the deep strange quiet, and holding to it, dwelling in that stillness, he saw life and death merge into one calm and shining sea that had no end.

HE WOKE BEFORE dawn and made them breakfast, then carried the pine box into the shed. Through the east windows the first gray light came as he laid the box down and brought hammer and nails. Then slowly and carefully he hammered the lid shut and the pounding of the nails rang out like solemn drumbeats in the winter dawn. As he drove the last nail in, he heard Ben at the shed door.

Laski opened the door for the old man standing there on snowshoes, a ragged cigarette in his mouth. "I'll be right with you," said Laski, gathering up his pick and shovel and his own snowshoes.

"We should dig the hole first," said Ben. "And you can come back for the box."

Laski nodded and walked ahead, over the hard morning crust of snow which crunched beneath their snowshoes. He went into the woods, past the skeleton of an old barn, where a porcupine had made his own beat in the snow, and Laski's path crossed it, and went down, into the deeper trees.

He followed an old logging trail through the pines, and Ben kept close behind him, smoking and coughing in the still morning air. The trail went through alder bushes, and down, to the larger trees, where no lumber had been cut for many years. Laski went on, through the old trees to the high bank above the stream. There the bank sloped down, with thin firs growing on its sides. Below was the stream, frozen but still flowing and the sound of its flowing came up to his ears. He stopped in a square of four small spruce.

They shoveled off the snow, clearing a space of earth in the little square. "The ground doesn't appear to be frozen," said Laski.

"No, it'll be good digging," said Ben, raising the pick. When he'd loosened the dirt, Laski shoveled it and threw it into a pile. The sky remained gray, and the hole took shape and grew deeper, Ben chopping and Laski shoveling out the loosened earth.

"Don't appear to be many roots," said Ben.

"No, it's not bad."

"Has to be wider though," said Ben. He broke more surrounding earth and Laski shoveled it off, so that he was able to climb down into the hole and work at the walls.

"How deep do you want it?" asked Ben.

"So an animal won't dig it up."

"Nothing will touch it," said Ben, but they shoveled deeper until Laski was in up to his waist, throwing the dirt out.

"You go and bring the box back down," said Ben. "I'll get the hole squared up."

Laski climbed out of the hold, put his snowshoes on, and followed the beat back up through the pines. The dampness of the morning brought many smells into the air, of dead wood and leaves, and from time to time he caught a faint trace of the musk of some animal who had passed by. All around in the snow were rabbit tracks weaving in and out through the trees, and there were also the tracks of a bobcat going in his gracefully curving line deeper into the forest, to the cedar bog, where the deer stayed.

The old barn came into view, and Laski went past it, toward the cabin. At the shed, he removed his snowshoes and stuck them in the snow. He entered the shed and laid the toboggan down on the floor, placing the little coffin on top of it. Then he roped it down.

When it was securely fastened, he went into the cabin. Diane was sitting up on the couch. "Did you find a nice spot?"

"On the high bank above the stream," said Laski. "I'm taking him down there now." He returned to the shed, and carried the loaded sled out into the snow. He put his snowshoes on again and took the rope in his hands. The load was very light and went smoothly over the crust.

On the slope behind the old barn, the toboggan moved on its own and he ran alongside it, guiding it with the rope through a stand of young spruce. The arms of the little trees touched the box, shedding some needles upon it, and a few tiny cones,